This book belongs to ....
.... ------------------------------------

The Kincaid's book of

Witches Goblins Ogres and fantasy

DERRYDALE BOOKS
New York

Copyright © 1980 by Brimax Rights Ltd.
All rights reserved.

This 1982 edition is published by Derrydale Books,
distributed by Crown Publishers, Inc.,
by arrangement with Brimax Rights Ltd.
First published in Great Britain by Brimax Books.

Printed in Hong Kong by South China Printing Co.

Library of Congress Cataloging in Publication Data
Main entry under title:

The Kincaid's book of witches, goblins, ogres,
and fantasy.

Reprint. Originally published: Cambridge,
Cambridgeshire : Brimax Books, 1980.
Summary: Thirteen stories including "Raiko
and the Goblin," "The Giant Stones," and "A
Queen's Revenge."
1. Fairy tales. 2. Children's stories.
[1. Fairy tales. 2. Short stories] I. Title:
Witches, goblins, ogres, and fantasy.
PZ8.K54 1982 [Fic] 82-9599
ISBN 0-517-392089
hgfedcba

A CONTEST

Once there was a farmer who had three sons. One day he called them together and said,

"One of you must go into the forest and cut some wood so that we can sell it and pay off our debts."

"Yes Father," said the three sons, each one waiting for the others to do something.

It was finally agreed, after a lot of arguing, that the eldest should be the one to go.

He was in the forest, lifting his axe to make the first cut, when a troll came up behind him and tapped him on the shoulder.

"Cut down any of my trees and I will kill you," said the troll, as pleasantly as though he was saying "Good morning".

The eldest son shivered from head to toe at the sight of the troll. He dropped the axe and ran home as fast as his legs would take him.

"I've j-j-just s-s-seen the troll," he gasped.

"Afraid of a troll!" scoffed his father. "When I was young no troll frightened me enough to make my hair stand on end!"

On the third day, Boots, the youngest of the farmer's three sons, said he wasn't afraid of any troll and he would go into the forest.

"You!" laughed his brothers, "just you wait till you see the troll. You'll run faster than we did."

Before he set off, Boots asked his mother to make him some cheese. When it was ready, he put it in a linen bag and tied the bag to his belt.

"What! Back already?" said the farmer.

"Th-th-there's a troll in the forest."

"Afraid of a troll!" scoffed the farmer. "When I was young no troll frightened me enough to make my teeth chatter!"

The following day the second son went into the forest. He had only been gone an hour when he came running back, looking as pale as a ghost and with his hair standing on end.

7

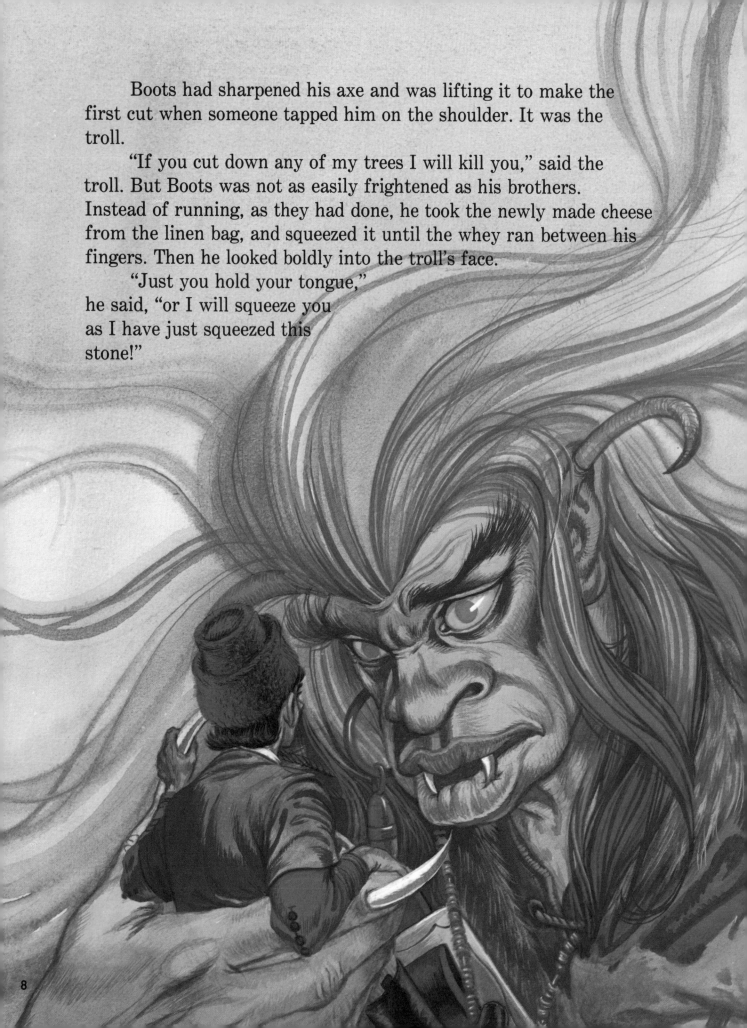

Boots had sharpened his axe and was lifting it to make the first cut when someone tapped him on the shoulder. It was the troll.

"If you cut down any of my trees I will kill you," said the troll. But Boots was not as easily frightened as his brothers. Instead of running, as they had done, he took the newly made cheese from the linen bag, and squeezed it until the whey ran between his fingers. Then he looked boldly into the troll's face.

"Just you hold your tongue," he said, "or I will squeeze you as I have just squeezed this stone!"

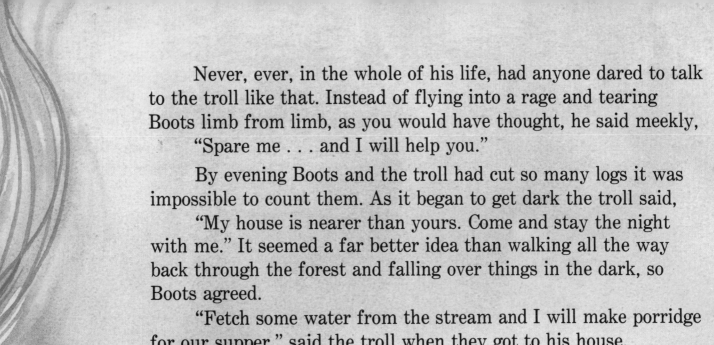

Never, ever, in the whole of his life, had anyone dared to talk to the troll like that. Instead of flying into a rage and tearing Boots limb from limb, as you would have thought, he said meekly,

"Spare me . . . and I will help you."

By evening Boots and the troll had cut so many logs it was impossible to count them. As it began to get dark the troll said,

"My house is nearer than yours. Come and stay the night with me." It seemed a far better idea than walking all the way back through the forest and falling over things in the dark, so Boots agreed.

"Fetch some water from the stream and I will make porridge for our supper," said the troll when they got to his house. "The buckets are beside the door."

Boots had already seen them. They were big enough for him to bathe in. He might have been able to lift one when it was empty, but he certainly wouldn't be able to carry it when it was full. He had to think quickly.

"I'll bring the stream in," he called boldly. "Then you will have as much water as you need."

"You can't do that," said the troll in a panic. "Think of the mess it would make. I've got a better idea. You make up the fire and I will bring the water."

When the fire was burning brightly the troll made porridge. There was enough bubbling in the pot to keep Boots and his two brothers fed for a week.

"Let's have an eating contest," said Boots. "I'll wager I can eat more porridge than you can."

The troll looked at Boots. He looked down at himself. He looked at the pot full of thick stodgy porridge. This would be a contest he couldn't lose.

"Why not!" he said, and took two plates to the pot and filled them both to the brim. He didn't see Boots put the linen bag under his coat and arrange it with the open end under his chin.

"Let's begin," said Boots, and picked up his spoon. For every spoonful of porridge Boots put into himself, he put four into the bag under his coat. Very soon his plate was empty and the bag under his coat was bulging.

"More please," he said.

The troll was amazed. "Are you sure you've got room?" he asked, looking at what he thought was Boot's round, fat, tummy.

"Of course I have," said Boots.

"Don't you feel just a little bit full?" asked the troll doubtfully.

"No," said Boots, and without so much as a blink, or a wince, he stuck his knife through his coat and into the bag which was hidden under his coat. The bag went flat as the porridge dribbled onto the floor. "Now I've got plenty of room," said Boots, and held out his plate for another helping.

When the troll had finished his second plateful, and Boots was half-way through his third, the troll put down his spoon and sighed. "I can't eat any more," he said.

"Do as I did and make a hole in your stomach," said Boots.

"But doesn't that hurt?" asked the troll.

"Did you see me wince? Did you hear me cry out?" asked Boots. The troll had to admit that he hadn't.

And so the troll did as Boots had done, but with one big difference. He hadn't got a linen bag hidden under his coat. So that was the end of the poor old troll.

Boots took home all the silver and gold he could find and paid off his father's debts and he never ate another spoonful of porridge as long as he lived.

RAIKO AND THE GOBLIN

Raiko was one of the richest men in all Japan. He was also the meanest. He had servants to look after his house and gardeners to look after his garden. The only thing he ever gave the poor was the scent from his garden. He wouldn't have given them that if he had been able to stop the wind blowing it in their direction. On a mountain ledge overlooking the valley where he lived, there lived a goblin. The goblin had the power to listen to people's thoughts, and one day, when he was sitting on his ledge, he saw Raiko walking in his garden and listened to what he was thinking. Raiko was looking for ways to save money.

'What use is a garden to anyone?' he thought. 'No one can eat flowers, and gardeners have to be paid. I'll dismiss them. And while I'm about it I'll dismiss the servants too. Why should I pay them wages when I can live in one room and look after myself?'

Raiko made the goblin very angry for he had given no thought to what would happen to the people he dismissed. Some of them had served him and his family all their lives.

That night Raiko couldn't sleep. He felt very hot, and uncomfortable, which wasn't surprising for he kept all his gold in a belt tied round his waist. He wore it everywhere, even to bed. He tossed and turned.

'I must have a fever,' he thought. 'I need someone to look after me if I'm going to be ill. I'll wait until I'm feeling better before I dismiss the servants.'

On the third evening of his strange sickness, which didn't seem to be getting any better, he had a visitor. The visitor was dressed in a long brown robe and Raiko had the uncomfortable feeling he could see right inside his head.

"You are very ill," said the visitor, as his shadow danced across the wall in the flickering lamplight. "It's a wonder the demon's haven't come for your soul already."

Weak though he was from lack of sleep, Raiko raised himself on his elbow and shouted loudly for his servants.

"Show this man out . . . at once!" But the servants didn't come running in answer to his call, the visitor stayed.

"There is a remedy for your sickness," said the visitor, as Raiko shrank back onto his pillow. "Loosen your belt. There is famine in the valley. Use your gold to feed the poor and you will be able to sleep."

"What!" shrieked Raiko, reaching under his pillow for a knife which he always kept there. "How do you know about my gold? I won't let you steal it!" He threw the knife at the visitor with every intention of killing him. But he was weak and his aim was poor. The visitor was only scratched.

The visitor leant forward and blew out the lamp. His voice rang out in the darkness like a bell of doom. "If you take no heed of what I say then you must die!"

Raiko shrank back in terror. There was a moon shining
outside and a shaft of eerie light fell across the dark room.
Raiko screamed. There was a huge hairy monster, with many legs,
creeping across the room towards him. It crept closer . . . and
closer. Raiko screamed again. A scream full of terror and
pleading. He could feel the monster's eyes burning into his very
heart when his servants came bursting into the room.

"Master! Master! What is it?" they cried. Their eyes
were on Raiko. They did not see the monster sink to the floor
and slide from the room.

Two of the gardeners saw the trail of blood it left and followed it out of the garden and up the mountain to a small cave. Sitting in the mouth of the cave was an enormous spider.

"Tell your master to loosen his belt, or I shall come and strangle him with it," it said.

But there was no need, for on their return the gardeners found Raiko weeping with remorse. "But for my servants I would have been killed," he said. He was a changed man. He vowed to look after all those who had served him, and to give half his gold to the poor.

After that, whenever the goblin looked down at the gardeners working in the beautiful garden on the hillside and at the well-fed children playing in the valley, he would touch the tiny scar on his cheek, and smile.

THE GIANT STONES

Once there was a shepherd boy who always took his sheep to graze on a high and windy plain. On a clear day he could see for miles whichever way he looked. In one direction was the village where he lived. In another was a distant winding river. And standing right in the middle of the plain, where the wind never stopped blowing, there was a circle of giant stones. No one knew how they had got there. The village people were afraid to go near them for there were tales that they were giants who had been turned into stone as a punishment. They were the only shelter the shepherd boy had when the wind blew icy cold, or the rain swept across the plain in torrents. They cast the only shadow when the sun was scorching hot. The shepherd boy was not afraid of them. He even, in time, came to look upon them as his friends.

Living in the same village as the shepherd boy was a sorcerer who could understand the language of animals and birds. One day he overheard two birds talking outside his study window.

"Have you heard . . ." one of them was twittering. "This Midsummer Eve, at midnight, the stones on the plain will rise from their pits and go to the river to drink."

"And have you heard . . ." twittered the second bird, "that there is treasure in the pits where the stones stand?"

"And have you heard . . ." said the first bird, "that if anyone takes the treasure it will turn to dust unless they give the stones a human sacrifice in return?"

The sorcerer rubbed his hands with glee, and began to plot. The treasure was his for the taking. But what could he do about the human sacrifice? The only person in the village who had no family to ask awkward questions when he disappeared was the shepherd boy. It would have to be him.

stones, he began to think differently. 'It would be very unfair to steal the stones' treasure when they are drinking and unable to protect it,' he thought. 'I will not do it. I don't care if I stay poor all my life. I will not do it.'

There was a rustling in the brambles beside him, and to his astonishment a strange child with furry ears and bright black eyes appeared.

He went in search of the shepherd boy, and after swearing him to secrecy he told him all that he had overheard. All, that is except one very important detail. He said nothing about the human sacrifice.

"We'll meet on the plain at midnight," said the sorcerer. "And when the stones go to drink we will have treasure beyond our wildest dreams . . . now remember, not a word to anyone."

At first, the shepherd boy was as excited as the sorcerer at the thought of the treasure, but later that day, as he was sitting in the shade of Old Mighty, the biggest of the seven

19

"You are right in what you think," said the strange child. "It would be wrong to steal from the stones, but they are your friends and give you leave to take some of their treasure. But first, you must cut a long trail of honeysuckle and lay it beside Old Mighty, and you must only take treasure from Old Mighty's pit."

On Midsummer Eve, the sorcerer and the shepherd boy went to the circle of stones and lay in wait for midnight. Just before the magic hour clouds covered the moon. Moments later the earth began to tremble. The stones were stepping from their pits. It was an awesome sight. Were they really enchanted giants? They began to move across the plain, rocking gently from side to side on invisible feet.

Presently there came the sound of a distant rumble. It grew louder. The stone giants were returning from the river.

'I must get out of this pit or I will be squashed under Old Mighty,' thought the shepherd boy and tried to climb out. The sides of the pit were slippery and steep. He couldn't find a foothold anywhere. He could hear the sorcerer screaming with fear.

"Quick!" cried the sorcerer, "We haven't got much time!"

The shepherd boy jumped into the pit from which Old Mighty had stepped. He gathered enough treasure to fill one of his pockets. In a nearby pit the sorcerer was shovelling treasure into sacks as fast as he could. And all the time he was shovelling he was thinking, 'No one will miss the shepherd boy . . . no one will miss the shepherd boy.'

The shepherd boy resigned himself to certain death. He looked up at the sky for the last time and saw the strange child with furry ears, peeping over the rim of the pit.

"Take hold of this," called the strange child, and lowered the trail of honeysuckle which the shepherd boy had cut and laid beside Old Mighty earlier in the day. "I will pull you up . . ."

It was a very close thing. As the shepherd boy fell gasping onto the grass Old Mighty stepped into the pit with a heavy thud. All around there were echoing thuds, and then, when the earth stopped trembling, complete silence. It was as though the stones had never moved.

The sorcerer was never seen again. The shepherd boy became a rich landowner, and though he never took sheep to graze on the plain again, he was often seen leaning against Old Mighty with a far-away look in his eyes.

MY-OWN-SELF

Peter would not go to bed when his mother told him to. He was naughty about most things, but about going to bed he was very naughty indeed.

He lived with his mother in a lonely cottage. There was nothing around it but moorland. It was a cheerful enough place during the day with bees buzzing in the heather and birds singing and twittering in the gorse bushes, but at night it was different. Sometimes it was eerie and still. Sometimes the wind seemed to be full of whispers. Peter's mother didn't like it. As soon as it was dark she would make up the fire and go to bed. She felt safe in bed. If anything happened, (it never had, but she was never certain it wouldn't) she could put her head under the blankets and pretend she wasn't there.

"It's time for bed, Peter," she would say as she put fresh logs on the fire.

"Time for you maybe, but not time for me," he would say cheekily. And he would stay up until he wanted to go to bed. Sometimes he stayed up half the night.

One night the wind was whispering round the house and Peter's mother felt sure there were fairies about.

"Time for bed, Peter," she said, even earlier than usual.

"Time for you, but not for me," Peter said. She pleaded. She grumbled. She shouted. Nothing she said made any difference. Peter sat toasting his toes in front of the fire and refused to move. At last she lost her temper.

"Well, I'm going to bed," she said, and she went.

Peter heard the bed creak as she got into it, and then the house fell silent, except for the crackling and spitting of the logs burning on the fire, and then that stopped too.

Presently there was a fluttering in the chimney . . . and an elf child jumped down onto the hearth.

"What's your name?" asked Peter, not in the least afraid, though he had never met an elf face to face before.

"My-Own-Self," said the elf child. "What's yours?"

"Just My-Own-Self too," said Peter, thinking if an elf child could give a funny answer, then so could he.

"I've come to play," said the elf child.

"Oooh good!" said Peter. "Now I can stay up all night."

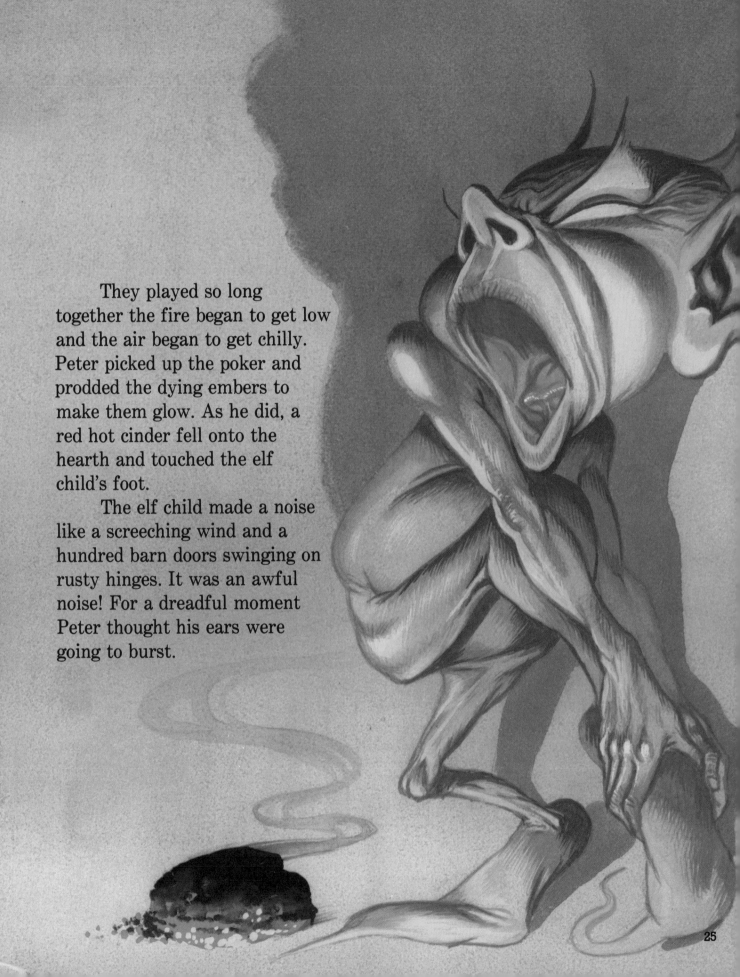

They played so long together the fire began to get low and the air began to get chilly. Peter picked up the poker and prodded the dying embers to make them glow. As he did, a red hot cinder fell onto the hearth and touched the elf child's foot.

The elf child made a noise like a screeching wind and a hundred barn doors swinging on rusty hinges. It was an awful noise! For a dreadful moment Peter thought his ears were going to burst.

Peter felt, rather than heard, that someone, something, was coming down the chimney in answer to that dreadful scream. He dived under the bed and crouched as close to the wall as he could.

"Who is there? What is wrong?" called a voice.

"It's My-Own-Self, and my foot's burnt!" cried the elf child.

"Who did it?" asked the voice angrily. Peter knew he had. He could see the angry face of an elf mother looking from the chimney.

"Just-My-Own-Self-Too" said the elf child, meaning Peter.

"If you did it yourself stop making a fuss," said the elf mother, not understanding at all. She reached out and caught hold of the elf child by his ear and yanked him up the chimney.

Peter crouched under the bed all-night long, afraid to come out. Next evening, when his mother said "Time for bed, Peter," he went straight away. He was afraid the elf mother might discover who 'Just-My-Own-Self-Too' really was, and come looking for him.

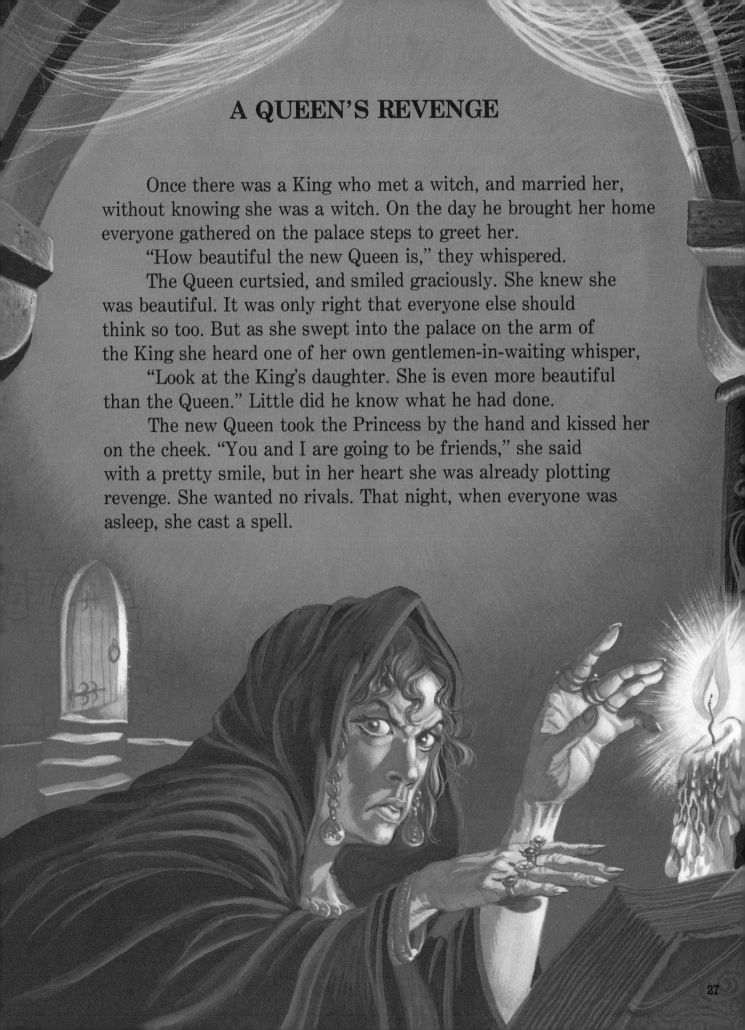

A QUEEN'S REVENGE

Once there was a King who met a witch, and married her, without knowing she was a witch. On the day he brought her home everyone gathered on the palace steps to greet her.

"How beautiful the new Queen is," they whispered.

The Queen curtsied, and smiled graciously. She knew she was beautiful. It was only right that everyone else should think so too. But as she swept into the palace on the arm of the King she heard one of her own gentlemen-in-waiting whisper,

"Look at the King's daughter. She is even more beautiful than the Queen." Little did he know what he had done.

The new Queen took the Princess by the hand and kissed her on the cheek. "You and I are going to be friends," she said with a pretty smile, but in her heart she was already plotting revenge. She wanted no rivals. That night, when everyone was asleep, she cast a spell.

Early next morning the palace echoed with loud screams. The maidservants who had gone to help the Princess to dress were running about, weeping and wailing and wringing their hands.

"What is it . . . what is it?" cried the King, who had come running in with his crown all askew.

The weeping maidservants pointed to the Princess's room.

What a dreadful sight met the King's eyes when he entered. Lying on the Princess's bed, with its head on the pillow was an ugly, scaley monster. There was no sign of the Princess herself. The poor King fell into a swoon, and while the maidservants did their best to revive him, the monster crawled unnoticed, from the bed, and from the palace. It dragged itself to distant rock and there it stayed.

The countryside was soon in terror, for hunger drove the monster to devour everything that crossed its path. When a wizard was consulted he said, "Tell the King to give the monster the milk from seven cows every day to appease its hunger . . . and tell the King his daughter will not be avenged until his son returns." The King's son was hundreds of miles away on an expedition, but the news travelled fast and when he heard what had happened the Prince swore to avenge his sister. He and his men built a long boat, with a special keel made from an ash tree, and set course for home.

The Queen's magic powers warned her that the Prince was coming. She summoned her imps. "Raise a storm!" she ordered. "Sink the boat! The Prince must not set one foot on land!"

The imps raised a storm which made the fish think there had been an underwater earthquake, but it made no difference to the long boat. Its ash keel protected it from the imps' magic and it rode the rough sea as though it was on a calm mill pond.

"I'm not beaten yet!" cried the Queen, when the imps reported back to her. And she cast a spell that made the monster go to the harbour entrance.

"The very person he has come to avenge shall be the cause of his death," she laughed cruelly.

The long boat was just pulling into the harbour when the monster lashed the sea with its tail and drove it back the way it had come. Each time the long boat drew close to the harbour the monster drove it back . . . again. . . and again. . . and again. The men in the long boat grew exhausted in their fight to reach the shore and at last the Prince ordered them to put back to sea.

The Queen, who had been watching the struggle, laughed, and went back to the palace where she pretended to be full of concern for the missing princess.

"What a comfort you are to me in my sorrow," sighed the King, who had been completely deceived.

The Queen wouldn't have smiled so prettily if she had known that instead of going right out to sea the long boat had gone round into the next bay. With no imps, and no monster to hinder them they landed easily. The Prince drew his sword, determined to find the monster and kill it.

"It tried to keep me from my sister," he said. "It shall die."

But the moment the Prince set foot on land, the Queen's power over the monster vanished, and when the Prince found it, instead of putting up a fight, it lay quietly on the ground. The Prince raised his sword and was about to plunge it into the monster's neck, when it spoke, with his sister's voice.

"Give me kisses three.
Though I am a poisonous worm
I will not harm thee."

'This is some trick,' thought the Prince, and would have struck the death blow there and then, but before he could strike, the monster spoke again.

"Give me kisses three.
Though I am a poisonous worm
I will not harm thee."

The Prince hesitated, then quickly kissed its cheek. The third time he kissed it, there was a soft hiss and the monster turned into his sister. He had broken the spell.

What a joyful procession it was back to the palace. How gladly the King greeted his two children.

"Now we are a family again," he said, turning to the Queen.

"My dear, what is wrong?" he asked, when he saw how pale she was.

"Watch this, Father," said the Prince. He touched the cowering Queen with a magic ash twig, against which a witch has no power, and she shrank and shrivelled until she became a fat ugly toad. So then the King knew he had been deceived and banished her from his kingdom for ever.

THE SPIRIT IN THE BOTTLE

Once there was a woodcutter who worked and saved all he could so that he could send his son William to school. But times were hard and the day came when all the money he had saved was spent and his son had to return home.

"Do not worry, Father," said William. "I will come into the forest with you and help you cut wood. We will be able to earn enough to keep ourselves."

"How can you help me?" sighed the woodcutter. "You are not used to such work . . .besides, I've only one axe. We are far too poor to buy another."

"We'll ask our neighbour to lend us one of his until I can earn enough to buy one of my own," said William.

The next day they went into the forest together. William was young and the work was new to him. He enjoyed every minute of it, and whistled and sang as merrily as any bird.

At midday the woodcutter said, "Time to rest."

"I'm not a bit tired," said William. So while his father sat under a tree and dozed, he went in search of birds' nests.

William climbed trees, looked in bushes and spied on birds sitting in their nests without disturbing any of them. He was looking for a way to climb into the branches of an ancient oak when he heard a voice calling, "Let me out! Let me out!"

"Where are you? Who are you?" called William, looking about and seeing no one.

"I'm at the foot of the tree," answered the voice. "Please let me out."

William poked about amongst the grass and dried leaves, and found a dirty glass bottle lying between two gnarled roots. He rubbed it clean on his sleeve. Sitting hunched inside it, with its knees under its chin was a tiny frog like creature.

"Hallo!" said William. "What are you doing in there?"

"Let me out and I'll tell you," it shouted, banging on the side of the bottle with its tiny fist.

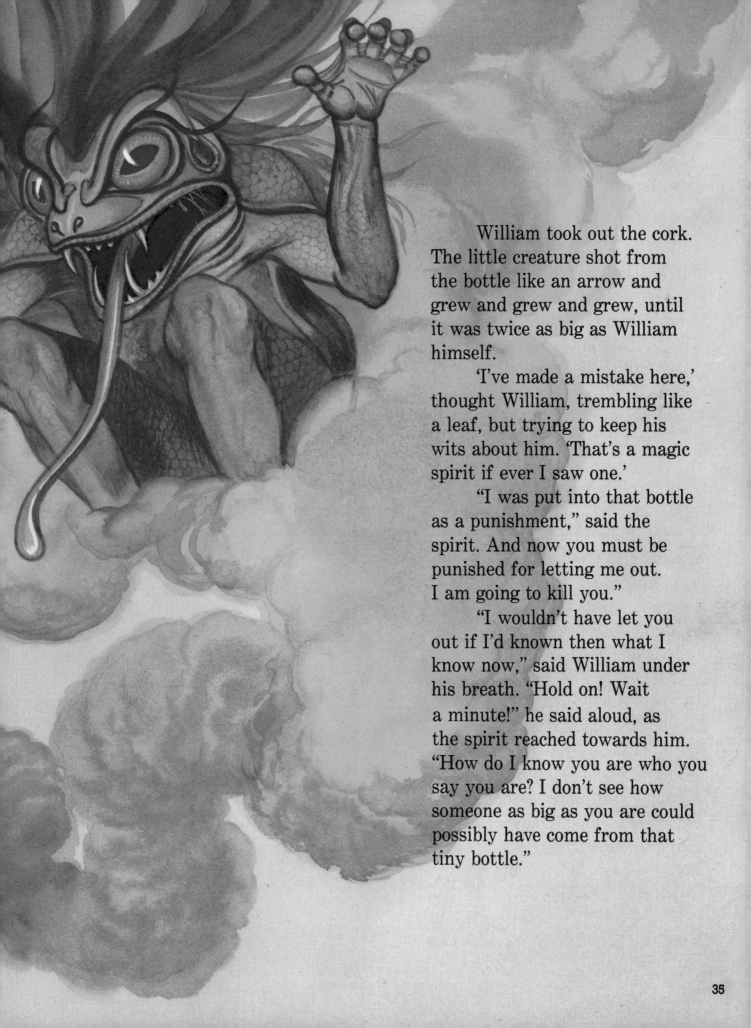

William took out the cork. The little creature shot from the bottle like an arrow and grew and grew and grew, until it was twice as big as William himself.

'I've made a mistake here,' thought William, trembling like a leaf, but trying to keep his wits about him. 'That's a magic spirit if ever I saw one.'

"I was put into that bottle as a punishment," said the spirit. And now you must be punished for letting me out. I am going to kill you."

"I wouldn't have let you out if I'd known then what I know now," said William under his breath. "Hold on! Wait a minute!" he said aloud, as the spirit reached towards him. "How do I know you are who you say you are? I don't see how someone as big as you are could possibly have come from that tiny bottle."

"Oh, don't you!" said the spirit. "Then I'll prove to you that I did." Whereupon he shrank to his former size and crawled back into the bottle.

"Got you!" shouted William and pushed the cork in.

"Let me out!" shouted the spirit in a fury. "LET ME OUT!"

"I'm not silly," said William. "If I let you out you will kill me."

"No I won't . . . I promise I won't," said the spirit. "Please, let me out."

William knew he was taking a risk, but he decided to chance his luck. He held the bottle at arm's length and took out the cork. The spirit was so grateful to be free again it gave William a piece of cloth that had the power to heal any wound, and turn iron and steel into silver.

When William returned his father said crossly,

"You will be far too tired to work this afternoon."

"I'm not tired at all," said William, and secretly rubbed the axe with the magic cloth. It turned the blade to silver, but silver isn't sharp like steel and the first blow he struck with it turned the edge up.

"Now look what you have done you foolish boy!" cried his father. "You have damaged our neighbour's axe. Now I shall have to pay for a new one."

When they got home William said he would ask the blacksmith if the axe could be repaired, but instead of going to the blacksmith he went to the silversmith. The silversmith gave him a small bag of gold in exchange for the axe.

When William next saw his father, he said, "Ask our neighbour how much he will take for his axe."

"I already have," sighed his father. "It's more than I have."

"Give him twice what he asks," said William, and showed his father the bag of gold.

And then, William told his father about the bottle he had found in the wood and the gift the spirit had given him. From that day, William and his father lived in comfort and because William used the magic cloth wisely, he became a very famous doctor.

ONCE THERE WAS A FOREST

A giant can change the look of a place as suddenly as any earthquake. Once there was a forest. It stretched for miles and miles beside the sea. It was home to many shy, wild creatures, and to two giants, though it was little more than a thick carpet to them.

Though giants are big, and strong, there is always someone, somewhere, who is brave enough to challenge them to a contest.

One of the giants who lived in the forest was tired of being challenged. He wanted to be able to eat his breakfast in peace, without having to get up every five minutes to answer the door to another Jack-the-Giant-Killer.

One day he said to his wife, "Wife, we are going to build ourselves a stronghold."

"Are we?" answered his wife with a sigh that nearly blew the birds out of the trees. Any plan of her husband's usually meant a lot of hard work for her.

"We will build it with white granite," said the giant.

"Where in the world will we get white granite from?"

"From the quarry on the far side of the forest."

"And who will carry the granite from there to here?" asked the giant's wife, though she knew the answer already.

"You will of course. I shall be busy building."

"Can't we build it with greenstone? There's plenty of that right here, and besides, it's not so heavy."

"I want my stronghold built with white granite!" said the giant with a scowl that made his wife think of sour lemons, and told her clearer than any words that it was no use arguing.

It takes a lot of anything to build a stronghold big enough to protect a giant, and granite is very heavy.

The giant's wife trudged backwards and forwards across the forest carrying boulders in her apron and getting more and more tired with each step. Backwards and forwards. Backwards and forwards. The giant built boulders into walls far quicker than she could carry them . . .after all, he only had to put one boulder on top of another.

"How slow you are!" he kept saying.

"I'm tired."

"How can you be tired? I'm not tired."

"That's because you have time to doze," she grumbled.

"That's because I get my work done quickly."

"You're not walking as much as I am."

"Stop complaining! Walking is easier than building."

"You wouldn't say that if you were doing it." The giant's wife thought it most unfair.

The next boulder she brought was very awkward. It made her arms ache and she was afraid it would tear her apron. She had already torn the hem of her skirt and scratched her ankle on a dead tree. When she heard the giant snoring like a swarm of giant bees, she thought, "He'll never notice if I get greenstone and put it amongst the granite."

She was tiptoeing past him with an enormous greenstone boulder hidden in her apron when he woke.

"That's greenstone you've got in your apron!" he shouted, jumping up in a rage. "I suppose you thought I wouldn't notice. Take THAT for being lazy!" He lifted his foot and kicked her. She stumbled! Her apron string broke! The greenstone boulder fell! It was so huge, and it fell with such a thud, it made a hole into which the whole forest fell.

"Now look what you've done!" grumbled the giant as water swirled in from the sea and filled the hole. "You've made my feet wet!"

"Serves you right!" said his wife.

YALLERY BROWN

One night, when the moon was shining and stars were twinkling, Tom went for a walk across the moor. It was so quiet he could hear the rabbits whispering in their burrows. Presently he heard another sound. Someone was crying. It sounded like a baby. Tom searched amongst the bushes and could find nothing, and then he heard a voice saying,

"Oooh, the stone! The great big stone! Oooh, the stone is on top of me!"

"That's no baby," thought Tom. He poked about in the grass with a stick and came upon a large flat stone half hidden by weeds and moss. He felt afraid, but he just had to look underneath it. It was very heavy, and very awkward but at last he managed to pull it up onto its end.

Underneath the stone was a scooped out hole, and lying on his back in the hole was a tiny little man. His wrinkled skin was as brown as a nut, and he had long, shining yellow hair. He blinked as the moonlight shone onto his face, then got to his feet.

Tom stood and stared.

"Close your mouth," said the little man in a voice that sounded as old as the world itself. "There's no need to be afraid. I will not hurt you. You've been kind enough to help me and so I shall help you."

"Wh.wh.who are you?" gasped Tom.

"I am Yallery Brown," said the little man. "Now for your reward. Would you like a wife to look after you?"

"I have a mother to look after me," said Tom. "But I would like some help with my work."

"Very well," said Yallery Brown. "But remember this. If you ever thank me for anything I do, I will disappear, and you will never see me again. Call 'Yallery Brown. . .come from the moors. . . I want thee', if you need me for anything, and I will come."

Before Tom could answer Yallery Brown blew a puff of dandelion seeds into his face, and when Tom could see again, Yallery Brown had gone.

Next day, Tom's work was done for him. The stables were swept. . .the horses groomed. . .the buckets filled. Whatever the master told Tom to do was done before Tom could lift a finger.

"Now I can laze in the sun whenever I want to," said Tom. He climbed to the top of the haystack and lay on his back and watched the clouds float by.

It wasn't long before the other stable boys noticed Tom was always walking around with his hands in his pockets. They couldn't understand how he was getting his work done so quickly.

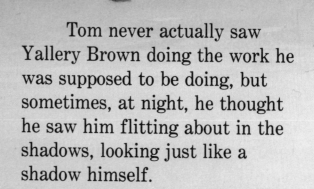

Tom never actually saw Yallery Brown doing the work he was supposed to be doing, but sometimes, at night, he thought he saw him flitting about in the shadows, looking just like a shadow himself.

Lazing in the sun, doing nothing at all, tends to get boring after a time, even for someone as lazy as Tom, and one day he decided he would do some sweeping. He picked up the yard broom. It jumped from his hands. . . and swept the yard by itself.

He tried to fill the buckets. They went to the tap and filled themselves.

When he tried to push the wheelbarrow it ran away from him and wheeled itself across the stable yard.

Tom was beginning to find it all a bit scary. . .and so were the other stable boys. There were invisible hands at work. They didn't like it. They went to their master and told him what they had seen. He didn't like it either. He said Tom must leave and find work elsewhere.

45

"I'll never get work anywhere all the time Yallery Brown is helping me," grumbled Tom, who by this time really did want to work. "YALLERY BROWN!" he shouted. "COME FROM THE MOORS! I WANT THEE!" He felt someone tweek his leg. He spun round on his heels. There was Yallery Brown, looking up at him, and grinning all over his nut-brown face.

"I'll thank you to leave me alone Yallery Brown!" shouted Tom. "I don't want anymore of your help."

"Ho, ho," laughed Yallery Brown. "You thanked me. . .I told you not to."

"Go away! Go away! I don't care if I don't see you again!" shouted Tom, stamping his foot in a fit of temper, and not a bit grateful for all the help Yallery Brown had given him.

Yallery Brown stopped smiling. "And now I will tell you something else," he said sternly. "I said, if you thanked me you would never see me again, and nor you shall. . . but. . ." Tom's heart sank. There was something about the way Yallery Brown said 'but' that he didn't like. ". . .but I didn't say I would leave you alone. With me as a friend you could have done anything, but you have behaved foolishly and I shall treat you like a fool."

Tom wanted to run, but his legs wouldn't move. Yallery Brown began to circle round him. Faster . . . and faster he went, till his yellow hair wrapped itself round him like a scarf and then he spiralled into the air like a dandelion seed caught in the wind and disappeared.

From that day onwards nothing went right for Tom. Although he never saw Yallery Brown again, Tom knew it was Yallery Brown's invisible hands that were responsible for all the mischief.

"If only . . ." he used to sigh. "If only I had left that stone unturned." But by then, of course, it was too late.

DIGGING FOR FISH

One starry night, when the fishermen were getting their boats ready to go out to sea, an old woman hobbled along the beach towards them pulling a spindly-legged boy by the hand.

"What do you want old woman?" asked the fishermen. "Can't you see we are busy? We don't want to miss the tide."

"Take my boy with you and teach him how to fish," she said.

The fishermen took one look at the boy, who had arms like broomsticks, and laughed out load.

"You can't be serious," they guffawed. "Him. . .a fisherman! A fisherman has to battle with the sea. HE couldn't do battle with a kitten."

"Please. . ." said the boy. "I'm stronger than I look."

"Get out of our way," they said roughly. "We haven't time to waste on the likes of you."

The boy picked up one of the nets lying on the sand.

"Leave that alone!" shouted the owner and cuffed the boy's ear.

"Take the boy home old woman," jeered the fishermen. "Fishing is mens work. . .leave it to the men."

"Mens work is it!" screeched the old woman. "Well, you'll catch no fish till you bring me that!" And she pulled off the silver thimble she was wearing on her thumb and threw it onto the sand.

One of the fishermen bent to pick it up. His fingers would not close round it. It was burying itself in the sand.

It was at that awful moment the fishermen realised what they had done. They left their nets and their boats and began to dig into the sand with their hands.

"Have pity on us. . ." they pleaded. "Have pity on us. . ."

But their pleas were in vain. They are digging to this day. Their boats are neglected and falling to pieces. Their nets are tangled and rotting. All because they dared to laugh at a witch and jeer at her son.

THREE GOLDEN HAIRS

Once there was a poor man whose only son was born under a lucky star. It was foretold that, one day, he would marry the King's daughter.

The King was very cross when he heard the news. "A poor boy like that marry my daughter! NEVER!" he said. He went to see the boy's father.

"I want to buy your son," he said.

The King was told the boy was not for sale, but he nagged, and argued, and pleaded, till at last the boy's father thought, 'My son can come to no harm with the King. He will give him a better life than I can. . .I must let him go.'

The King carried the baby off. But instead of taking him home to the palace, he put him in a box and cast the box adrift on the river. With any luck it would float out to sea and the baby would never be seen again. Marry his daughter indeed!

The boy hadn't been born under a lucky star for nothing. The box was fished from the river by a miller. He took the baby home to his wife and they brought him up as their own son. He grew into a fine strong lad, full of mischief, but kind too.

One day, the King happened, just by chance, to call at the mill.

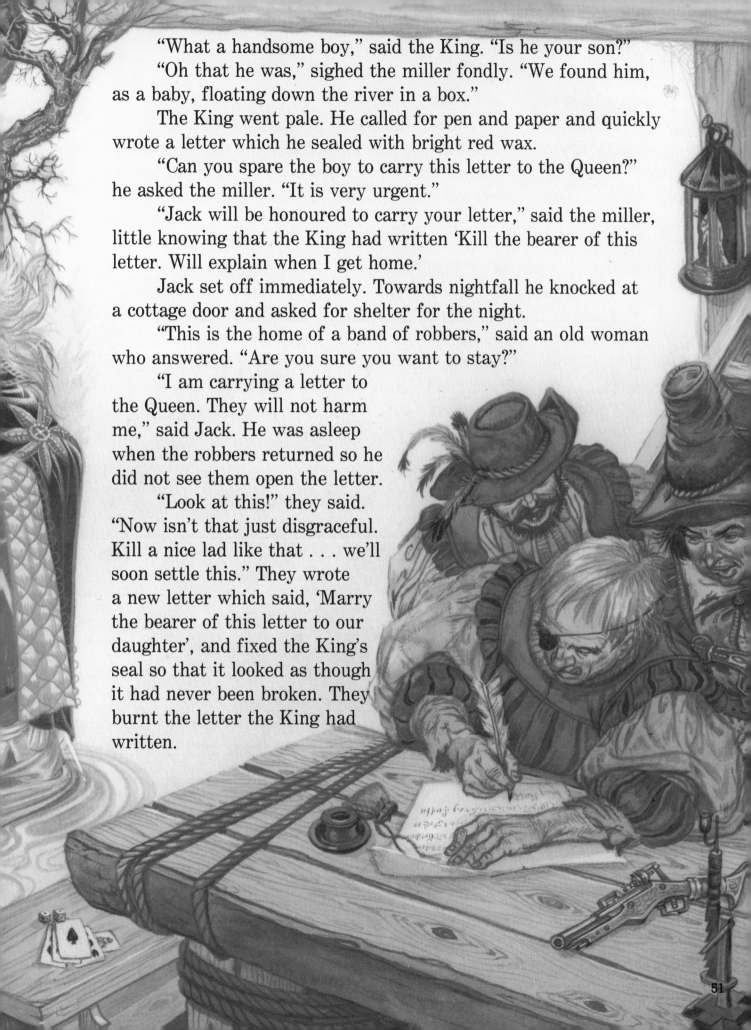

"What a handsome boy," said the King. "Is he your son?"

"Oh that he was," sighed the miller fondly. "We found him, as a baby, floating down the river in a box."

The King went pale. He called for pen and paper and quickly wrote a letter which he sealed with bright red wax.

"Can you spare the boy to carry this letter to the Queen?" he asked the miller. "It is very urgent."

"Jack will be honoured to carry your letter," said the miller, little knowing that the King had written 'Kill the bearer of this letter. Will explain when I get home.'

Jack set off immediately. Towards nightfall he knocked at a cottage door and asked for shelter for the night.

"This is the home of a band of robbers," said an old woman who answered. "Are you sure you want to stay?"

"I am carrying a letter to the Queen. They will not harm me," said Jack. He was asleep when the robbers returned so he did not see them open the letter.

"Look at this!" they said. "Now isn't that just disgraceful. Kill a nice lad like that . . . we'll soon settle this." They wrote a new letter which said, 'Marry the bearer of this letter to our daughter', and fixed the King's seal so that it looked as though it had never been broken. They burnt the letter the King had written.

51

Jack continued his journey next day without knowing that the letter had been changed. He was very pleased to marry the Princess when the Queen arranged it.

When the King returned and found he had a new son-in-law he was very angry. "If you want to stay married to my daughter you must bring me three golden hairs from the head of the giant," he thundered, thinking secretly that the giant would soon put an end to Jack.

Jack set off at once. The guard at the gate of the first city he passed through asked him if he knew why the fountain in the market place had run dry. "I will give you an answer when I return," said Jack. The guard at the gate of another city asked Jack if he knew why a tree which had once borne golden apples no longer bore even a leaf. "I will have an answer for you when I return," said Jack.

The ferryman who took him across the lake asked how he could escape from the ferryboat and gain his liberty. Once again, Jack said he would give an answer on his return.

When Jack reached the giant's cave, the giant was not at home. "What do you want from him?" asked the giant's grandmother.

"Nothing very much," said Jack boldly. "Just three golden hairs from his head."

The giant's grandmother frowned. "That could be very risky," she said. "I'd better help you. But first you must hide." She turned Jack into an ant and hid him in her apron.

While they were waiting for the giant to come home Jack asked the grandmother if she knew why the city fountain had run dry.

"I do not," she said, "But I'll ask the giant if he knows."

"Will you also ask him why the tree which used to bear golden apples bears them no longer, and what the ferryman must do to gain his liberty?" asked Jack.

"I can smell boy!" said the giant when he got home. "Where is he?" But Jack was well hidden and the giant wanted his supper so he soon gave up looking.

After he had eaten the giant lay his head in his grandmother's lap and went to sleep. It wasn't long before he was snoring.

The grandmother tweeked one of the golden hairs from the giant's head.

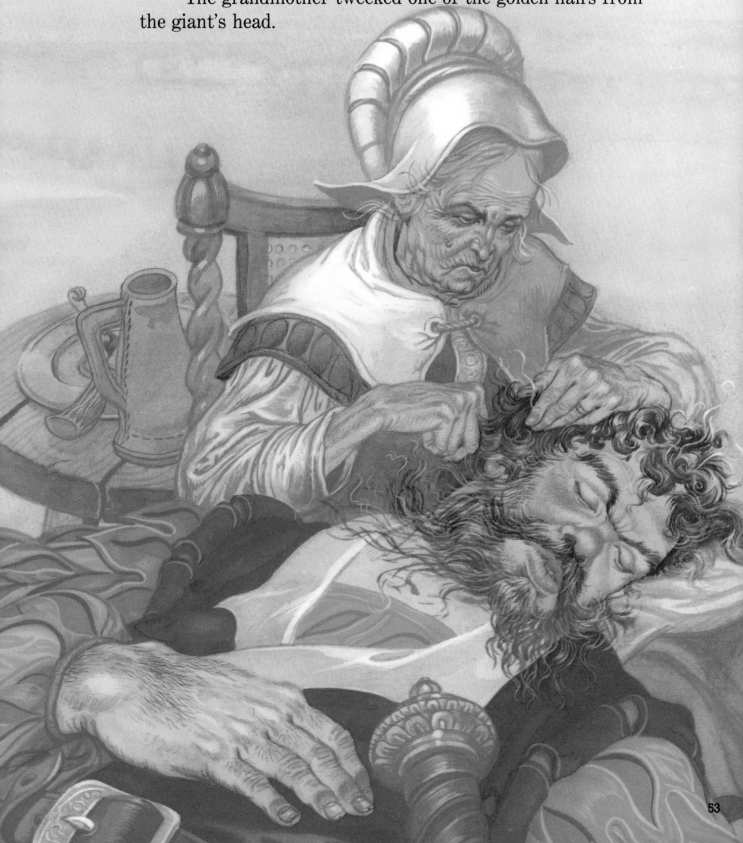

"What was that?" cried the giant, waking up with a start.

"Nothing dear," said the giant's grandmother. "I was dreaming of a fountain which has run dry. Why would a fountain run dry dear?"

"Because there is a toad sitting under it," said the giant who knew the answer to almost everything. "Kill the toad and the water will flow again."

As soon as the giant closed his eyes the giant's grandmother tweeked out another of his hairs.

"Ouch!" cried the giant. "What was that?"

"Nothing dear," said the giant's grandmother. "I had another dream, that was all. Now why should an apple tree that used to bear golden apples bear them no longer?"

"There is a mouse gnawing at the root. Kill the mouse and the tree will bear fruit again," yawned the giant sleepily.

The giant's grandmother thought it better to wait a while before she pulled out the third hair.

"Ouch!" said the giant when she did. "I suppose you've had another dream?"

"Yes, I have. How did you guess?" she asked. "Now tell me, what must the ferryman do to gain his liberty?"

"Give the rudder to another passenger of course," sighed the giant. "Now will you let me get some sleep?"

"Of course dear. I won't disturb you again, I promise," she said.

The next day, when the giant's grandmother had turned Jack into himself, he set off for home.

Jack waited until he was safely across the lake before he told the ferryman how he could gain his liberty and when he answered the questions the city guards had asked, he was richly rewarded with gold and silver.

The King had to smile and pretend to be pleased when he saw Jack, for not only had Jack brought the three hairs, he was now very rich. The Princess really was pleased to see him.

It so happened that the King himself was the next person to cross the lake. The ferryman handed him the rudder. The King is ferrying passengers to this day, which probably serves him right. Perhaps, one day, Jack will tell him what he told the ferryman.

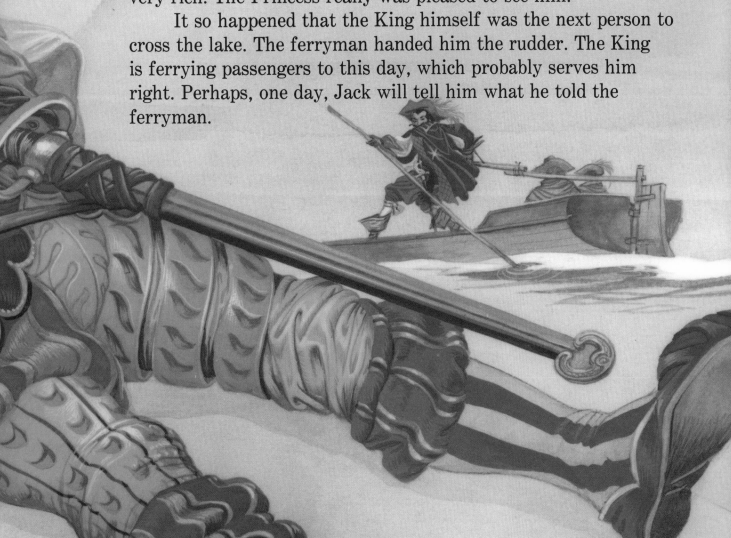

PIXIE OINTMENT

Once there was a fisherman and his wife who were friendly with the pixies. The pixies never teased them, or plagued them as they did other people. Whenever the fisherman and his wife did the pixies a favour they were handsomely rewarded.

"The pixies must be very rich," said the fisherwife. "I wonder how they come by their money."

"You might well ask," said her husband. "There's more goes on around here than meets the eye."

One night, some pixies brought a sick pixie baby to the fisherman's cottage.

"Please nurse our baby until he is well again," they said, handing the tiny bundle to the fisherwife. It was the first time either of them had seen a pixie baby. One of the pixies gave the fisherwife a small box.

"What's this?" she asked, taking a peep inside.

"It's ointment for the baby's eyes," he said. "Put a little on his eyelids every morning. Be sure not to forget. It's very important."

"I won't forget," she said.

"A word of warning," said the pixie. "If you put any of the ointment on your own eyes you will go blind."

"Ooooh! I wouldn't do a thing like that," said the fisherwife. "I'm surprised you should think such a thing."

"We'll come back for the baby in a few days," said the pixie. "Make sure you remember what I said."

"I will," said the fisherwife. She made the pixie baby a cradle from a pie dish, and tucked it round with thistledown to keep it warm.

On the second morning, when she had put the ointment on the baby's eyelids, she couldn't resist dabbing a little on her own.

"What are you doing?" cried her husband in alarm. "You know what the pixie said."

"Well, say it he might have done, but it hasn't made a scrap of difference to me," said the fisherwife. "I can see just as well now as I could before. You worry too much, husband. The pixies wouldn't harm me."

"How can you be so sure?" said her husband, looking very worried. "There's more goes on around here than meets the eye. . . you mark my words."

"Don't be such an old fuss pot," laughed the fisherwife.

The sick baby was soon well again. When the pixies came to take it home they asked for the box of ointment.

"Did you put any on your own eyes?" asked one pixie who took the baby.

"No! No, of course I didn't," said the fisherwife as though butter wouldn't melt in her mouth. Her husband gasped.

"Then we'll bid you good day," said the pixies.

"What nice little folk they are," said the fisherwife when they had gone.

"There's more goes on around here than meets the eye," said her husband looking very glum. "You mark my words!"

"I do wish you would stop saying that," said the fisherwife irritably.

Next market day, the fisherwife met her sister at the crossroads and they went into town.

"Isn't it busy today?" said the fisherwife.

"No more busy than usual," said her sister.

"No wonder," said the fisherwife. "The pixies are here. I've never seen them at market before. Oh. . .oh. . .the rascals! They are taking things and not paying for them! They are stealing! Did you see that! That was wicked! Did you see him take a coin from that purse?"

"I don't know what you're talking about," said her sister. "Pixies! What pixies? I see no pixies! You are imagining things!"

"I'm not! Look! you must have seen that! And that . . . and that . . ." The fisherwife spun around on her heels pointing in all directions. Suddenly she pounced on the pixie who had brought the pixie baby to the house. "You rascal!" she said, wagging her finger at him crossly. "Just you put those apples back!"

"Who are you talking to?" asked her sister, looking very bewildered.

"She cannot hear us, or see us, and you shouldn't be able to either," said the pixie. "You lied when you said you had put no ointment on your own eyes. I warned you. You should not have meddled in what doesn't concern you." He blew on her face. The fisherwife, who had seen more than she should have seen, could see nothing at all. Then she wished she had listened to her husband's words.

THE CHASE

In Iceland there once lived an old man and an old woman who were very poor. They had part of a cottage to live in, and a piece of a field to grow things in. They had one son called Karl, and one cow called Bu-cola, and that was all.

One morning, when the old woman went to milk Bu-cola she could not find her. She had disappeared without trace. There wasn't so much as a hoof mark to show which way she had gone.

"Oh, Bu-cola, where are you?" sobbed the old woman. "We shall starve without your milk."

Karl wiped his mother's tears away with the end of her apron.

"Do not cry," he said. "I will go and look for Bu-cola. I will not return until I have found her." He put some food into a knapsack and set off.

At mid-day, as he sat eating his bread, he thought, 'The world is a very large place. How am I going to find Bu-cola? I could be walking in the wrong direction.' He was doing up his knapsack when he had an idea. He wondered why he hadn't thought of it before. He stood on the largest rock he could find, and called as loudly as he could,

"Moo if you are alive Bu-cola. Moo now!" And then he put his hand to his ear and he listened.

Very, very faintly, far, far away to the east he heard an answering moo. Even at that distance he thought he knew the sound.

Karl walked until his legs grew tired, then rested again. When he was refreshed, and ready to continue, he called,

"Moo if you are alive, Bu-cola! Moo now!"

The answering moo was very much closer.

"I'm coming Bu-cola!" shouted Karl, and hurried on until he came to a deep gorge. He stood so that his toes were almost hanging over the edge, than called again.

"Moo if you are alive, Bu-cola! Moo now!"

This time the answering moo was loud and clear and came from somewhere beneath his feet. Bu-cola was in the gorge. Karl slipped and slithered his way to the bottom and found a cave. Inside the cave, tethered to a stake, was Bu-cola.

"Moo!" said Bu-cola, as glad to see Karl as he was to see her.

Karl untied her and led her up the side of the gorge.

"Now for home," said Karl when they had got to the top and recovered their breath. "Mother will be glad to see you."

They hadn't gone very far when there was the sound of something heavy thudding and thumping behind them. Karl looked back over his shoulder to see what it was, and nearly died of fright. They were being chased by a gigantic troll wife and her troll daughter. They looked very angry. 'That cave must have been theirs,' thought Karl. 'They must think I've stolen Bu-cola from them. They must be coming to get her back!'

"Oh dear, what shall I do?" he cried aloud. "I'm no match for a troll wife."

"Moo!" said Bu-cola. "Pull a hair from my tail and lay it on the ground behind us."

Karl did so at once. This wasn't the time to be asking why, or what for.

"Oh hair of my tail become a deep river that no one can cross!" mooed Bu-cola. Immediately the hair became a raging river, with Karl and Bu-cola on one side of it, and the troll wife and the troll girl on the other.

"Fetch me my great ox!" shouted the troll wife. The ox was a magic one. It drank the river as though it was no more than a puddle. Then, of course, there was nothing to stop the troll wife and the troll girl following Karl and Bu-cola.

"They're getting very close," panted Karl, as the ground shook and trembled beneath their feet.

"Pull a hair from my tail and lay it on the ground behind us!" mooed Bu-cola. "Oh hair of my tail, become a raging fire that no one can cross," she mooed, the instant the hair was on the ground. A wall of leaping flames hid the troll wife and the troll girl from view but it did not hide the sound of the troll wife's voice as she shouted for her ox.

The great ox spat out all the water it had drunk and put out the fire.

"Quicker! Quicker!" panted Karl. "The trolls are almost upon us!" The troll shadows had already caught up with them and were looming larger and larger.

"Pull a hair from my tail and lay it on the ground behind us!" mooed Bu-cola urgently. "Oh hair of my tail, become a mountain which no one can cross!" she mooed as it touched the ground. The hair turned into a mountain large enough to stop any troll.

The troll wife's voice rolled round the mountain top like angry thunder as she cried, "Bring me my husband's rock drill!"

"Are we never to escape. . ." gasped Karl. There was the sound of falling rock. Karl snatched a glimpse over his shoulder as he ran. There was a hole breaking through the mountain.

"She's crawling through . . . I can see her head . . ." gasped Karl. "Quicker! Quicker! I can see her shoulders . . ."

But this time the ground did not tremble and shake beneath their feet. This time there were no footsteps thudding behind them. This time there was no dark shadow blotting out the sun. The troll wife was shouting, but she wasn't shouting at them. She was shouting because she was stuck! Her head was sticking out of one side of the mountain. Her feet were sticking out of the other side. She couldn't go forward. She couldn't go backwards. Eventually she turned into mountain stone herself. The troll girl disappeared as though by magic: Karl and Bu-cola were safe.

SEEING IS BELIEVING

Once there was a wizard who sometimes left his secret room and went into the market place. He liked entertaining people with his tricks. They enjoyed it, and so did he.

"Roll up! Roll up!" he cried one day. "Come and see my magic bird!" It wasn't long before a crowd had collected.

"Come on then, show us what it can do!" shouted a boy who was carrying a plank of wood on his shoulder.

"Lend me your plank for a minute or two," said the wizard.

"It won't come to any harm, will it?" asked the boy.

"Of course not. Put it on the ground," said the wizard. He took a cockerel from a sack and put it on the ground beside the plank.

"Watch carefully," he said. He fluttered his fingers over the cockerel and chanted some strange words. To the astonishment of the crowd the cockerel lifted the plank with its beak and began to strut up and down with it.

"How can it do that?" cried the boy whose plank it was. "That's heavy. . .I know. . .I've been carrying it."

Oohs and aahs of astonishment swept through the crowd like a gust of wind.

A girl at the edge of the crowd stood on her tiptoes so that she could see better.

"What's clever about that?" she said. "Any cockerel is strong enough to pick up a straw!" The girl had a four-leaf clover in her hand and could see things exactly as they were. The wizard's magic had fooled everyone else, but it didn't fool her.

Her words were enough to break the spell, and then everyone saw that the cockerel was carrying a straw.

"Cheat! Cheat!" they shouted. The poor wizard, who had only been trying to entertain them, was pelted with cabbages and rotten tomatoes and chased out of town. How everyone laughed at his discomfort. The girl with the four-leaf clover laughed loudest of all.

The months passed, and then one day, there was a village wedding. The villagers were walking in procession across the fields, to the church where the wedding was to be held, when those behind tripped over the heels of those in front. The procession had stopped.

"What is it? What is happening?" asked the people at the back as they jostled to the front to see what was wrong.

They had come to a stream which was far too wide to jump across. There was no bridge over it, and no plank with which to make a bridge.

"We'll have to go back the way we have come, and take the long way round to the church," they cried.

"No! No, we can't do that. I'll be late for my wedding," cried the bride, who was the girl who had found the four-leaf clover.

"Then what shall we do!" they asked her.

In answer the bride kicked off her shoes. She bundled her skirt round her knees and stepped into the stream.

"Brrr . . . it's very cold," she shivered. "Ouch! It's very stony," she winced as she carefully stepped her way across.

"Do not get your wedding dress wet," called the onlookers, those that is, who were not running as fast as their legs would take them the long way round to the church. They began taking off their own shoes, and tucking up their own skirts. The men rolled up their trouser legs. Soon, everyone was wincing and shivering as they followed the bride.

"Where are your eyes that you think that is water?" asked a mocking voice.

All eyes turned towards the bank. They saw the familiar face of the wizard. All eyes looked downwards. Instead of water they were wading through grass and blue flax flowers. They were holding their shoes above their heads. They were all showing their knees. The wizard was having the last laugh, and now it was they who had the red faces. How foolish they looked and how foolish they felt.

THE DRUMMER

One evening a drummer boy was walking beside the lake when he saw three pieces of fine white linen. He took one of the pieces home with him and laid it across the foot of his bed.

That night, just as he was going to sleep, a voice said, "Drummer, give me my shift." He rubbed his eyes sleepily and saw a girl standing at the foot of his bed.

"I will, if you tell me who you are" he said.

"I am the daughter of a king. I have fallen under the spell of a witch. She lets me bathe once a day in the lake with my sisters. My sisters have gone but I cannot return until I have my shift." She picked up the piece of white linen.

"Wait!" cried the Drummer. "Before you go, tell me how I can help you."

"You can free me from the witch if you can reach the top of the glass mountain, but that is impossible. Even if you find it the sides are too steep to climb."

"Where is the glass mountain?" asked the Drummer.

"All I can tell you is that the road you must take goes through the forest where the giants live," said the girl, and then she went.

As soon as it was light, the Drummer took the road leading through the forest. He beat loudly
on his drum which roused a giant who had been lying asleep in the grass.

"What are you drumming for, you impudent boy?" demanded the giant, who didn't like being woken so rudely.

"To show the way to the thousands who follow me."

"What do they want in the forest?" asked the giant.

"To kill you, and all like you," said the Drummer.

"Don't be foolish," laughed the giant. "We giants will trample you like ants."

"We will creep on you like ants when you are asleep and hit you with steel hammers," said the Drummer.

The giant didn't like the sound of that at all. "Stop drumming," he said, "and I'll do anything you ask."

"Carry me to the glass mountain," said the Drummer.

"I can only take you part of the way," said the giant. "My two brothers will take you the rest."

The giant's second brother carried the Drummer to the foot of the glass mountain. It was three times as high as an ordinary mountain and quite impossible to climb.

"If only I was a bird," sighed the Drummer. He was sitting on a grassy hillock trying to work out what to do when he saw two men quarrelling over a saddle.

"You are stupid to quarrel over a saddle when you have no horse to put it on," he said.

"Not as stupid as you think," said the men. "Sit on this saddle and wish, and you can go wherever you want to go."

"Can you indeed!" said the Drummer. "Then let me settle your quarrel for you." He went a short distance and put a stick in the ground. When he returned he said, "Whoever reaches the stick first wins the saddle."

As soon as the men began to run the Drummer sat on the saddle and made a wish to himself.

Suddenly he was at the top of the glass mountain where there was a little house, a fishpond and a pine forest. He knocked at the door of the house. An old witch who opened it said she would give him food and a bed for the night if he would perform three tasks for her.

The Drummer's first task was to empty the pond with a thimble, and sort the fishes. He worked hard, and long, but the water in the pond never seemed to get less. Towards evening a girl came from the house and spoke to him.

"You look tired," she said. "Lay your head in my lap and sleep. When you wake your task will be done."

When the Drummer was asleep the girl twisted the ring on her finger and made a wish. The water rose from the pond in a fine mist and floated away. The fish jumped about and sorted themselves.

When the Drummer woke, the girl said, "When the old witch asks why one fish is lying by itself, throw it at her and say, 'That one is for you, old witch'."

The Drummer did exactly as the girl told him. The witch said nothing, but she looked at him very strangely.

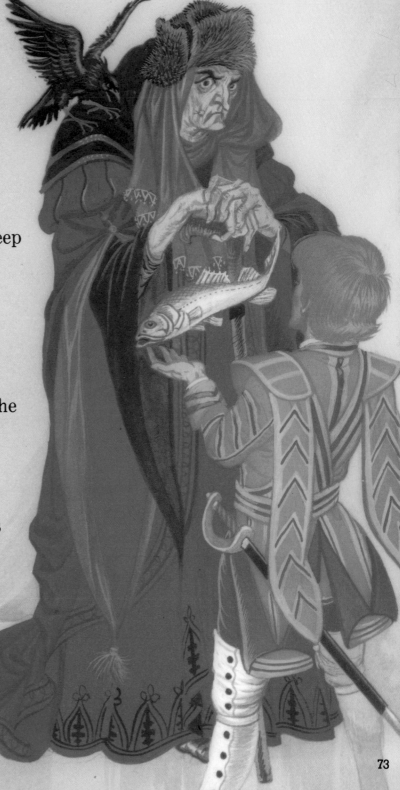

The Drummer's second task was to cut down all the trees in
the forest and split them into logs. An impossible task, even
with a sharp axe, and the axe the witch had given him was blunt.

At midday the girl came from the house, and said, "You
look very tired. Lay your head in my lap and sleep."

When the Drummer woke he found the second task completed.

"When the old witch asks why one log lies apart from the
others," said the girl, "give her a blow with it and say, 'That
is for you old witch!'"

The Drummer did exactly as he was told. The witch looked
at him very strangely, but she said nothing. The third task she
set him was to pile all the logs together and burn them in one
huge fire. The girl came from the house and once more
told him to sleep. When he woke the flames were leaping and the
logs were burning fiercely.

"You must do whatever the witch tells you to do without
fear," said the girl before she went back into the house.

The witch came and watched the flames leaping and curling.

"Look," she said. "There is a log right in the middle of
the fire which is not burning. Bring it to me."

The Drummer jumped, without fear, into the heart of the fire and brought out the log. As the log touched the ground it turned into the girl who had been helping him. Then he saw that she was the Princess he had come to rescue.

"You shall not have her!" screeched the witch, and leapt forward to push her into the flames, but the Drummer was quicker than the witch. It was the witch who fell into the flames, not the Princess. That was the end of the witch!

The Drummer and the Princess filled their pockets with treasure from the witch's house and went home.

"Do not kiss your parents on the right cheek when you greet them," said the Princess. "If you do, you will forget me."

In the excitement at being home the Drummer kissed his parents on both cheeks, and all memory of the Princess faded from his mind.

The Princess did not forget the Drummer. When she heard a marriage had been arranged for him she wished for a dress as golden as the sun. She took it to the palace which the Drummer had built with his share of the witch's treasure.

"What a beautiful dress," sighed the girl who was to be the Drummer's bride. "Oh, I do wish it was mine."

"I will give it to you if you will let me sit outside the Drummer's room tonight," said the Princess.

The girl wanted the dress so much she agreed, but before the Drummer went to bed that night, she gave him a sleeping potion.

During the night the Princess opened the door to the Drummer's room and called softly,

"Dear Drummer, are you awake?"

The Drummer was sleeping so soundly he did not hear her and she went sadly away.

The next day she wished for a dress as silvery as the moon, and went to the palace. The bride-to-be agreed to let the Princess spend another night outside the Drummer's room in exchange for the dress, but she made sure he drank another sleeping potion before he went to bed. Once again he slept soundly and did not hear when the Princess called.

On the third day the Princess wished for a dress that glistened like the stars. The same thing happened, but that night the Drummer did not drink the sleeping potion. When the Princess called softly, "Dear Drummer, are you awake?" he heard her. The sound of her voice was enough to restore his memory.

"You are my true bride," he said.

So, there was a change in the wedding plans. The Drummer married the Princess. As for the girl who was to have been his bride, she had the three most beautiful dresses in the world, so they all lived happily ever after.